THE MINER
STORIES
BOOK FOUR

BLACK THUNDER: The MINER BOOK 4

S.E. McKenzie

DEDICATION
To the miners everywhere who should have been safer.

CONTENTS

CHAPTER 1

March 15th 2031, around 10:00 AM:

"What do you mean we have a rat infestation?" Mayor Stern screamed as he banged his coffee cup on his desk. "Who is responsible for this?"

"No one will say sir. Some blame you. I don't," Susan replied.

"Who is blaming me?"

"Everyone is, sir. They blame you for the air quality too, sir."

"Well, that is good news. Our air quality is second to none."

"Sir, our air quality is considered to be the worst on the continent."

"Susan everyone knows that I execute orders that are designed to win elections every four years. That is what I do. My staff are in charge of everything else. No one in their right mind would think that I could win if I were found to be…" Mayor Stern was not able to finish before John Bell interrupted to scold Susan for speaking.

"You should be taking notes. Your job description is to take notes. You are wasting our time talking about things you know nothing about."

"Actually the blogs and news websites are talking about nothing else. There is concern sir that the black clouds growing in the sky are toxic and could poison water sources in other locations. You should read some of those articles, sir. They are frightening."

"They are all fake; every single article is fake and written to agitate and to cause trouble," John Bell and Mayor Stern said at the same time.

"The rat problem is not that serious. There will always be rats in Pitville. We are located near several bodies of water and everyone is too busy to chase rats all over the place," John Bell said as he glared into Susan's eyes.

"How can anyone compare our air quality to big cities like LA and New York? How could they say our air quality, in the country of all places, is worse than theirs. The news story Government's Official Directors are demanding when every detail related to this morning's Cold Feet Mountain Rockslide. The report has to be filed immediately."

"How can we file a report that we haven't written yet? How are supposed to know what caused the rockslide in no one else does?" Mayor Stern grumbled. "The rockslide was an unexpected hundred second event. What can you say about something that happened in one hundred seconds?" Mayor Stern added.

"Well shit happens and the answer to many of the world's problems is depopulation. We have too many people everywhere. Our mechanized employees will be the most efficient and obedient workers in the industry. And as we depopulate we choose who survives. If we don't nature will do it for us," Alex Coaltonstone replied.

"All it took was one hundred seconds and all those people's lives and homes just vanished into rubble," Susan whispered as she held her coffee cup in both hands.

"Those people know that the chances for a long life are slim for them. Like Alex said, the way we are managing the population is much kinder than nature's way. We choose who goes. Nature attacks randomly. Those people can protest all they like but it won't change a thing; nature is the cruelest terrorist of all," John Bell said as he looked at Susan taking notes. "Susan, why are you taking notes of this private conversation that we are having?" John Bell asked as he stood up and read what she had typed then deleted it and sat back down.

"Don't you think that if we could have predicted a rockslide before it happened, we would have? This disaster has cost us a bundle. We didn't know this was going to or we would have located those homes further away from Cold Feet Mountain and the mine. And that is what we doing, now, as speak; we are arranging for relocation," Alex asked.

"We are also have a hell of a job protecting the bank site. Who knows what has been buried but crowds appearing to be digging up what they can and are running off into the woods like a pack of animals. This disaster is just a nightmare for security," John Bell said.

"It was common knowledge that the mountain was moving. The local legend is that Cold Feet Mountain walks and most of the locals won't live near it unless we force them to," Susan said.

"We don't know what caused the rockslide, Susan," Alex Coaltonstone interjected.

"And we don't know who or what is under the rockslide, either. Our advisors are advising us that it will be foolhardy to try to recover the dead," John Bell said.

"But they are recovering the loot at the bank site?" Susan asked.

"Not officially. We are being told that we will be better off just to leave the dead in peace," John Bell said before he began coughing uncontrollably.

"Our Big Seven Real estate committee is marketing the land that which is now free from those horrid houses those people were living in," Mrs. Stern said.

"For starters we will have to neutralize all the fake news stories that are being generated by liberals and protestors," Mayor Stern said as he tried to speak over the noise John Bell was making while blowing his nose.

"You see dear, 'look' is what is important; not just politics but in real estate and social climbing. Not that you would know anything about that, would you dear?" Mrs. Stern interjected. "Now take those awful miners. We feed them, and they gobble down their food as if there was no tomorrow. They are so rude. Those men have no concern for manners or decorum."

"It is so nice to have you here, Martha," Mayor Stern said to his wife.

"Welcome to our meeting, Mrs. Stern," Bob Campbell said as he inhaled from his green puffer.

"Thank you Darling. Thank you Mr. Bell."

"Miners are usually very hungry dear and now that the mines are closed…" Mayor Stern said

"The mines are closed because they are bringing in captive illegals to mine in chain gangs…" Susan said before Mayor Stern interrupted her.

"Why is everyone interrupting me? I am the mayor; I am supposed to be giving the permission to address me…"

"Why is everyone shouting? It is so rude," Mrs. Stern interjected again.

"I am sorry dear," Mayor Stern said sheepishly. "I didn't mean to sound like I was shouting at you, Honey. I thought I had made it clear that I was only shouting at Susan," Mayor Stern said as he glared at Susan.

"Apology accepted," Mrs. Stern said as she gave her husband a quick peck on each cheek. "This has been a lot fun but I must go shopping now," Mrs. Stern said as she sanitized her hands before she put on her white gloves.

CHAPTER 2

March 15th 2031, around 10:00 AM:

"Yes, I understand this is a matter for Child Welfare Services that is why I am requesting to speak to a real person at G.O.D.'s Child Welfare Services. We found a little girl, she looks around two or three, I am willing to be her foster mother and if her family can't be found I would like to adopt her. She says her name is Mary but she has been very traumatized. Her family has most likely been buried in the Cold Feet Mountain rockslide and she is sleeping in our hotel at this very moment. When we found her, she was hysterical, and drenched in mud. We have cleaned her up, and fed her. Mary needs stability and security right now. I know I could give her a great life full of travel, adventure and fashion. I just have to fill out the forms the right way so that all the pieces fit together exactly the way the Government's Official Directors intended. I don't know if Mary has any living family left. I know I could give her a far better than she could ever have staying here. The air quality here is awful. Even before the rockslide, the air quality was awful. The way the locals burn coal and wood to heat their homes you would think they had never heard of natural gas," Dianne said as she looked at Jackson for reassurance.

"Are you sure you are talking to a real person and not some bot, Di?" Jackson asked.

"No, I am not sure. I am never sure these days. The whole world is moving so fast, and I want to protect this baby so she can experience some normalcy,"

"Normalcy? With us?"

"You know what I mean."

"I am not a baby, I am a toddler, my brother David is the baby. He is in the hay. I want my mom and dad. Where are they? Mary said as she walked into the room.

"Oh sweet heart."

"Jackson get the door."

"I don't hear knocking. Oh I do now."

"Dianne, you look ravishing," James Coaltonstone said in his usual way.

"James Coaltonstone? What are you doing here? How did you find us?"

"Steve answered the phone when I phoned the PPZ to find out if you were okay and …"

"Can't you see we are busy, and I am on the phone," Dianne replied wishing James Coaltonstone would go away."

"And …" Jackson cued James.

"And I own this hotel."

"And…" Jackson tried to cue James again.

"And I wanted to apologize if I was responsible for our little twitter spat I am sorry. It was cruel, unnecessary and I mentioned some very private things too publicly," James confessed.

"And …" Jackson cued James some more.

"When I heard that terrible noise, I realized that the mountain was coming apart. As the rock slid and covered part of Coalton Two, I was devastated. I drove as close and as fast as I could to where you were staying to see if you were okay. I couldn't see where I was going so I had to turn back. Thank God that you were one of the lucky ones, Dianne, and managed to escape with your life. Even the bank was buried. Wealth that took generations to build just buried in less than four minutes," James said.

"God had nothing to do with it as far as I know. Jackson managed to get us out of there," Dianne said.

"I was driving blind. I couldn't see either. It was like we were driving through a huge black cloud," Jackson said trying to sound less shaky than he felt.

"That is exactly what it was like. That huge black cloud is covering the area. And I was making sure the rockslide had not buried you, or whatever it was."

"They are calling it the biggest rockslide ever. The whole side of the mountain came down. The locals said the mountain walks and some of them refused to work in it, which is partly why I had deportations waived for men who volunteered to pay off their debt to society."

"You mean the ones that are buried under all that rubble chained to each other?" Jackson asked?

"I lease those workers and that is all I know. So tell me how you got here in one piece."

"We managed, to get away right before the hotel was buried, thanks to Jackson, he drove us out of there in his horrible underwear and left all of his clothes behind."

"I did bring towels," Jackson said as Dianne looked at him in disbelief.

"I was so scared," Dianne said.

"That mountain slid on top of everything even the bank," James said.

"It sounded so angry," Jackson said

"James what are you doing?" Dianne asked as she watched James peck at his phone.

"I am ordering room service and I am getting Jackson some clothes," James replied. "You know Dianne; I actually thought you had been buried under the slide. When I heard that deafening roar I felt terrible that our last words said to each other were in anger," James said.

"I then realized it wasn't your fault when you spread fake news, you are just doing your job at PPZ. You put your 'all' in our job, just the way I do."

"Fake News! You call these factual disasters that occur one after the other, fake?" Dianne said trying not to shout.

"Without the media all these people under the rubble would be forgotten ghosts, we humanize what would be just described by G.O.D. as statistics."

"Who is this little girl? She is beautiful, James asked.

"We found her. I am on the phone. G.O.D.'s social service department has placed me on hold. I am offering to keep her if we can't hook her up with her parents and give her the best life I can. I never had time to have children of my own, which is one of my greatest regrets."

"Di, you can't do everything, you have covered hot spots that some of the bravest men at PPZ refused to go to. And you do humanize what would otherwise be just forgotten and filed away as statistics," Jackson said about to hug Di.

"What is it about you two?" James asked.

"Are we going to get food then?" Dianne asked

"I am not hungry," Jackson said.

"I meant for the baby."

"I am not a baby, David is the baby, I am the toddler. I want my parents," Mary cried as she walked into the room

"I know dear, we are going to pretend to be your parents for a while," Dianne said before she wished that she hadn't.

"My mom says I am not supposed to talk to strangers, I want my parents," Mary said.

"Well we don't have to be strangers; we can get to know each other. Your parents can't be here," Dianne said hoping she could soften her tone a little.

"When can they be here? When can we get David out of the hay?" Mary asked innocently.

CHAPTER 3

March 15th 2031, around 10:00 AM:

"I hate being a kid," Mathew said as he sat in Ashley Knight's makeshift office.

"Mathew, this is an incredible picture. You were just flyking into the black cloud and lit it up and found that baby girl sitting on top of all that rubble."

"Uncle James calls that luck."

"Well you have to settle down and have some breakfast. Then we must focus on your studies," Ashley Knight said.

"Everything shakes on this boat," Mathew complained. "I feel sick when I eat cause of all the shaking. Why doesn't my mother wake up. Is she going to die too? What is going to happen to Ginger Junior? Is he going to be okay?"

"Your brother will probably be okay. He may never be as strong as you, though. He was born very tiny and you must be brave and strong for him. So settle down and eat your breakfast and then do your homework."

"Why? Jackson says you can't get a job without experience, and you can't get experience without a job. Jackson says that the whole system is fixed. Uncle James says that too, in his own way."

"What do you mean?"

"Jackson and Uncle James both say the system is rigged. Jackson says the dream is for winners and nightmares are for the losers. Uncle James says that dreamers are losers too, the ones who own what they do are the only winners, ever."

"Sounds awfully simplistic to me."

"I just made another $10 K selling that picture of that little girl crying on the rubble where her house was. I have money but when I go anywhere I am followed by security as if I was going to rob every single store I walk into. I go into a restaurant and people ask me where my parents are. I tell them my dad is dead and my mum is sleeping. Uncle James said once you are rich the world is not so rigged cause money opens up doors.

"You know your little brother needs you to be strong and to focus on the positive.

"That is what I do. When I am flyking, I feel so good. Grandma says it is because I am closer to heaven when I am flyking."

"Your grandmother tells me that you are eating like a bird, not like a growing young man and she is very worried about you."

"I am not the only one who is feeling bad on the ground. When I flyke around, you would not believe all the garbage I see. There is junk dumped everywhere. The bush covers a lot of it up. Uncle James says that is the analogy and strategy of getting by on the ground, especially when it is near zero."

"You must settle down and eat now.

"Dr. Knight you should come flyking with me. Grandma loves it. Uncle James loves it. You would love it."

"When will I get the time to go flyking. All my time is spent on this ship. I must monitor your brother and your mother. They would not survive if something happened to the machines."

"I know that is the way it is now. But one day, we could go flyking together. You will see how great it is. Grandma is right, when we flyke we are closer to my dad. Me and Grandma can feel him near us."

"I understand Mathew. You have to do other things too. You can't just spend your life flyking. How will you earn a living?"

"How long am I going to live for?"

"No one knows." Ashley responded.

"All those people who were buried this morning while they were sleeping; what were they expecting to do tomorrow? Were they expecting to be dead? They are going to just leave them there. Uncle James says that it is too dangerous to get them out."

"You know Mathew, you have to departmentalize. What happens to some people is not part of your life. Those people are strangers. Most of those people buried are miners or related to

17

miners. They know and accept the risks that go with who they are. That is the way destiny works in this world. It is different for different people and has nothing to do with you."

"What about the deportees who were chained and could not get out."

"They were paying back their debt to society."

"Whose society?"

"No one owns a free society, Mathew."

"Are you sure?" Mathew asked.

"Couldn't you just do your homework and when your mom wakes up you can show it to her?"

"When will that be? Do you really believe that she is going to ever wake up again?"

"There is always a possibility of recovery as long as the machines that are supporting your mother are able to keep her alive."

"How long do you think it will be, before she wakes up?"

"I don't know. We will just have to believe that one day your mother will wake up. Mathew, do you really think your Uncle James is happy?"

"I think he is sad because my mom and my brother are so sick but yes, in his own way, I think he is happy because he is free because he is so rich and he does what he wants. He doesn't have to sit in one place for a long time and take orders from people like I have to do when I take classes with other kids. I don't see why I can't just listen to my lessons on audio-files while I flyke around taking pictures of real life. I find learning like that a lot easier. I sit in a chair, and you know I just can't get my head wrapped around ancient history lessons. Why would someone want to kill a president like JFK? Why keep those files secret until 2029, and then expect us, to remember things that they obviously wanted the public from that era to forget? I also don't understand the revolution. I mean it was supposed to be about freedom from the Tyranny that was experienced in the Old World but the wealth base back then relied on slaves."

"Mathew, what do you want for breakfast?"

"French fries and gravy and a muffin would be great and a can of Red Bull. That is what Uncle James has."

"I have ordered eggs, bacon, hash browns, toast and a glass of orange juice and a side dish of fruit. I will have the same."

"But you get yours with coffee and I don't, even though I am the one expected to adjust to this boring flat world, where there is one disaster after another. How am I supposed to stay awake without? Uncle James you are back."

"Yes just in time for breakfast and may I add my two cents Doctor Knight?"

"Certainly," Ashley replied.

"Mathew is right. I am going to go flyking with him after we eat breakfast. I could use some stimulation myself," James Coaltonstone interjected.

"Uncle James do you ever wonder what is under all the ice?"

"Of course I do, that is my job. I drill holes, to get what is under all this ice. What we mine pays for this ice breaker, our down suits, our gear, your baby brother's life support," James said.

"And Mom's too. How long do you think my mom will be asleep? Mathew asked.

"Not for long, I hope." Doctor Ashley replied.

"How come you get caffeine and I don't. Caffeine calms me down a little."

"Because, Mathew you have just turned 15 years old and you need more structure and no caffeine. You are wild enough as it is and you are eating like a bird. You are behaving exactly the way your grandmother says you do. You have been up most of night flyking. You saw things above the rockslide, which anyone would find very disturbing. But you, you took photos that were so graphic most media outlets would never be allowed to publish them."

"PPZ people gave me $10,000 for those pictures so why can't I celebrate and eat what I want and do what I want. Uncle James says I should celebrate. Uncle James says that in the end money is everything, nothing else matters as long as you have money in your pocket."

"Your Uncle James knows there are a lot of things that matter that money can't buy."

"Like what?"

"Life and love."

"Uncle James is keeping both my brother and my mother alive when the system would have let them both die Uncle James is keeping them alive until they are both strong enough again to live without life support."

"Well that photograph you took of that little girl crying on the rubble was awesome as a photograph but what do you think about it from an ethical point of view?"

"It is the truth. That is what Jackson says. My photographs are a moment of truth; nothing more and nothing less."

"That photo might make you famous overnight. It is an incredible shot. Possibly a one in a lifetime shot. And once you have experienced the excitement of fame you may find day to day life too drab and you might get left behind."

"It sounds more like the drabs are being left behind than me."

"You are impossible."

"People died this morning. They don't even know how many. People are dying all the time. Ginger is gone. My mom is almost gone. My little brother would have been gone if it hadn't been for Uncle James. And Uncle James says I am moving ahead. And I need that feeling of flyking in the open sky. Only time I feel free, Dr. Knight; is when I flyke. You know Uncle James promised to flyke with me again when he finds the time. He said that maybe in a couple of days we could go flyking together."

"That photograph you took of that little girl might make you famous, overnight, and you have to be very careful," Ashley warned.

"Why?"

"Because you are only fifteen and you have lost so much and you still have to find your place in the world."

"Well, I know, but why do I have to think about it or talk about it right now?"

"You don't, but deep down the memories will always be there. One day something irrelevant might trigger you to over-react and you need to understand that others won't understand. Your objectives can pull you forward. You need to finish high school, go to college. Try to have a normal life. Try to follow a normal schedule, and try to focus on what we have to do to conform to the world around us. I have to write reports, you have to finish that civic history lesson and send it back to your teacher."

"Well Pitville High isn't there anymore. Uncle James moved it to Coalton Valley 2, and was buried in the slide this morning, with everything else that was in the path of the rockslide.

"Send it to your teacher's email, they will figure it all out. You have stick to a routine that has some structure. You have to graduate from high school, and you probably will want to go to college, if not for you, for your grandmother, for James, for your mother,"

"Will my mother ever wake up?"

"There is no physical reason why she can't. She is on life support and is doing as well as expected,"

"And my little brother?"

"Actually he is doing really well," Ashley replied as she glanced at the crew member who was rolling the breakfast tray towards her.

"We need to work, and move forward," Ashley said.

"I just don't get why we have to think about civic history, when there are so many horrible things going on now. When I flyke I feel closer to my father and to Ginger that I ever do when I am stuck on the ground. When I play checkers with IQ I get confused. Sometimes I can feel Ginger speaking out to me. I don't know how or why. It is almost like part of Ginger is living in IQ," Mathew said

CHAPTER 4

March 15th 2031, around 10:30 AM:

"It is amazing how chaotic the world is outside the hotel, and how smoothly this hotel runs. Considering so many people are buried under rock, I feel very guilty sitting here, just relaxing, now that Mary is sleeping I can't help myself feeling guilty that we survived this and so many died so randomly.

"Maybe it wasn't random at all. Miners were laughing about how the mountain was mining itself," Jackson said.

"Jackson, why are we alive and all those other people aren't?"

"Because of my quick thinking; once you woke me up of course."

"Jackson! I am being serious."

"So am I. If we didn't escape we would have been buried alive just like everyone else. There is no reason to feel guilty for escaping. We were awake while most of the victims were fast asleep and probably were buried alive without ever knowing what hit them," Jackson said

"I wish I could find some meaning in all of this," Dianne replied.

"It means that life is short. That is what it means. Life sometimes is much shorter than we expect it to be. Sometimes life is longer, and then we grow old and watch our youthful selves die."

"Jackson, sometimes your sensitivity astounds me."

"Astounds me too. I am not usually this sensitive. The point is we escaped, we are alive. Maybe we can a difference, if only to

Mary. We could add some enjoyment to her life she might never be able to experience, once she is lost in the system."

"Will you marry me Jackson if they won't let me keep Mary as a single mom?"

"You don't need to ask. Of course I will marry you. Then we could adopt Mary if no one claims her and be a real family," Jackson replied.

"James, how many people do you think were buried this morning?" Di asked.

"Well houses are gone, so entire families must have been wiped out. A couple of miles of my new railway is buried under rubble. My mine is buried under the rubble and those illegals; we will never really know who they are gone. I lease them so G.O.D. will be demanding a report from me. We just took them down there to pay their debt to society and then we were going to send them back to Mina. Sometimes we just have to leave people where they are, depending on how dangerous the recovery effort is. But Dianne you survived, that is what matters," James said

"Tell me more about the prisoners that may be down there?"

"The Big Seven Coal Group leases the convicts and illegals from G.O.D.; usually when our lease expires we get a new batch of convicts and illegals and the old batch are sent back to Mina for harvesting," James said.

"Harvesting?" Are you joking?"

"Of course I am not joking. The organ trade is booming. There is a growing demand for young organs so why waste them. We feed them; we give them training and striped uniforms. Their identification number is tattooed on their forehead for visibility. We position them so they can work the coal seams while chained to each other so they don't run off. There will be a rescue mission of course. One of the crew from our freight train, which was just leaving my mine, scrambled through the rubble to warn the passenger train. Our communications were down, but we seem to be on line now. G.O.D. will take care of the necessary details and as far as we know the coal seam which leads to surface is being used by survivors to escape?"

"How could they escape chained in the mine like that?" Dianne asked.

"Good question. I really don't know. Those illegals found a way to get into our country they will find a way out, if there is a way. Have some more champaign dear," James suggested.

"It is too early in the morning for alcohol. Why are you trying to turn me into an alcoholic? Do you have any Red Bull?

"I will order some."

"Was there any warning?" Dianne asked

"You think I have some direct link to Mother Nature?"

"Well you seem to do pretty good with the ladies?" Jackson interjected.

"Jackson we are being serious," Dianne scolded.

"What is important is that you and Jackson escaped it and are here. Mary escaped,"

"Dianne are you sure you will not have some champaign. We must celebrate that we are alive and going to better and stronger than ever, without feeling any guilt for surviving. Guilt will only pull us back."

"That face on the bottle it looks a lot like you," Dianne said as she held the bottle."

"It is me Dianne. My face creates brand recognition for my newest brand of champaign that we are enjoying. Or at least I am. I wish you would join me."

"I have already told you it is too early to be drinking. I have lost a night of sleep," Dianne said.

"What are you planning to do about that little girl?"

"Dianne is thinking that she would love to adopt her and if worse comes to worse she will marry me to qualify," Jackson said.

"Are you kidding?" James asked, suddenly looking serious.

"I feel so bad for little Mary. Do you think she is really better off than all those people who lost their lives this morning?" Dianne asked, as she looked like she could use a drink of James' champaign.

"Absolutely, if she lives with you. You could give her a great life, Di." Jackson said.

"This hotel should be running smoothly, where is the Red Bull? I own this hotel and I don't tolerate any excuses for sloppiness regardless of what may be going on outside. This hotel is designed to feel and be a palace. Please have some champaign." James replied.

"What are you doing?" Dianne asked James before Mary walked into the room.

"When are we going to get my brother out of the hay? He will be really hungry by now," Mary asked.

"Oh Honey," Dianne said as she fought back tears.

"I am still waiting for G.O.D. to phone back, my marital status did not fit the form I had to fill out to be eligible to foster Mary," Dianne explained.

"I didn't know that you had a marital status, Dianne."

"I don't," Dianne replied.

"It is just a form, and if the form doesn't meet the standard the bots can't go to the next step before completing a previous step. It doesn't matter how important you are, to a bot you are just code," Jackson said.

"I know Jackson! You don't have to explain to me how these forms work. That is not the problem. I need to know how to get around it. I am single and may not qualify to foster Mary and I know I could give her a great life and I would make just as good a mother as anyone," Dianne said.

"I know, Di. We just might have to marry each other," Jackson replied.

"That is a fine idea. Why don't you two get married? If you want to foster Mary so bad, just follow the procedure and get it back on track. I built my empire knowing what rules I say that I follow. Nothing works by the book or script. You know that more than anyone; don't you Dianne?

"I suppose so."

"She wants her parents and her little brother, she really doesn't want us," Jackson said.

"And the locals are calling the fall of Cold Feet Mountain a sign of the End Time. Does that mean we should believe that life is finished for all instead of just for some. We are alive, we need to celebrate our lives by building the good especially when something bad happens.

"I think just moving ahead as if you are at the beginning instead of the end of something is less defeating and more energizing," Dianne said.

"Life with you would be a huge step up for Mary, Dianne," James said.

"If we don't do something to help her, Mary's life will only get worse, if that is actually possible. She will always be falling through crack after crack in the system," Jackson said.

"Not if I can help it," Dianne replied. "Social Services takes for ever to do anything. It seems like it is deliberate so that the child ages out of the system with as little expense as possible. I know it is all that the public has, but I know I could do so much more for her. I have seen enough disasters to know how everyone keeps getting torn down, not just by what happened to them, but by the process which is supposed to be helping them. It is like they have to conform to some perfect definition before they can act. No one seems to notice how cruel unintended consequences can be regardless of how good intentions are. Growing up without any personal power, without any person space, without any plans or expectations for the future," Dianne said.

"Well they don't want the wards of the state to have personal power. It gets too complicated that way. Treating everyone the same and confining them to the lowest of the low expectations works," Jackson said.

"Jackson," Di scolded.

"Jackson is right. Personal power to a degree creates personal happiness but it also creates all kinds of complications. Being dependant on G.O.D is all about giving up your privacy and can lead to all kinds of indignities and humiliations but it seems to simplify things for a lot of people. What do you think drives me, Di? James asked.

"Greed! My Dad says that greed drives you and he also says that you stonewall everything you can when it benefits you and you push things with reckless abandon when it suits you too," Mary said as she walked into the room.

"Jackson!"

"Mary, let us go for a walk," Jackson suggested.

"Jackson the air quality is terrible out there."

"I suggest the pool. We have paper swim suits in all sizes. And it is open every day no matter what. And it is even open after hours for our special guests. Which you are because you a VIP now," James said.

"What is a VIP?

"A very important person just like you," James replied as he kneeled on the ground Mary ruffled James' hair.

"My dad says your hair is fake," Mary said.

"As you see it is not, but now I will have to comb it over again," James said.

"Will my mom and dad be there?"

"Your parents are gone Mary. I am sorry," Jackson interjected.

"Gone where," Mary asked.

"Mary, just because some bad things are happening doesn't mean some good things can't happen too at the very same time. You just have to know how to make your own way and go with the flow. You will miss your parents, but you don't want to miss out on your youth or take it for granted," James advised.

"James, the child is only around three years old," Dianne interjected.

"Yes, and she has been at death's door. Mary, my stepson lost his dad and his mom is in a deep sleep, but he gets out and flykes. The doctor wants him to spend more time in class, to socialize with other kids. But it is not the same for him. People don't act the same around him. They feel sorry for him. The kids' parents remind him of the parents he doesn't have. But he doesn't give up, he loses himself in his passion of flyking and taking photos. When my stepson is flyking he is free and I am sure he feels one with nature, instead of struggling against it. The doctor is trying to condition my stepson to be normal, like other kids. But how can he be? He lost his innocence when he lost his parents. In this world you either rise or fall. My stepson rises above his hardship. When he flykes he can see things from the outside in, instead of from the inside out," James said.

"What are you talking about," Di asked.

"I understand," Mary said. "Can we go get my brother? He is still in the hay."

"Mary, I am being serious. People sometimes tell my stepson to not take photographs because they don't like it. My stepson takes photographs anyway. He takes photos of all the things that seem to be deliberately hidden from view like all the piles of dumped cars, stoves and fridges. When he flykes he has a bird's eye view of what is on the ground and he takes incredible photographs. If someone yells at him Mathew just flykes away," James said.

"Can we get my brother now? Mary asked again.

"Mary is a beautiful name. My first love's name was Mary. She died in a senseless accident," James said sadly.

"James, is that rumor true then?"

"I am not aware of any rumor that is true. That is why rumors are called rumors."

"James!"

"Dianne!

"You don't understand. My brother is in the hay and he is very hungry," Mary said.

"How old did you say this kid was?" James asked.

"I am three and David is one and he is in the hay. We have to go and bring him home," Mary said.

"I understand dear," Dianne said.

"No you don't. We have to get my brother out of the hay. He will be crying and he will be hungry."

"You are three, Mary. There is a lot that adults know that children don't know. Mr. Coaltonstone is right! We have to make the best of every opportunity that we have. And when you go swimming with Jackson I will be talking with Mr. Coaltonstone about adult things," Dianne explained.

"I want you to know, Mary that greed doesn't drive me, being a winner drives me," James said before Jackson interrupted him.

"What do you mean your brother is in the hay?" Jackson asked.

"I will show you," Mary said as she ran out of the door.

"Mary come back here at once," Dianne ordered.

"I will get her," James offered.

"I have to get my brother out of the hay," Mary screamed as James carried her back inside while she was waving her arms and kicking.

"Mary, you know that story I told you about my stepson?"

"Yes," Mary replied.

"People say he is taking an awful risk, flyking mostly alone. Sometimes taking photos of things some people would rather him not take photos of, but you know why we let him do things most kids are not allowed to do?"

"No," Mary looked interested and was beginning to calm down.

"We let him do these things because he is celebrating life as it slips by. Life is short. We never know when it will be our turn to go," James explained.

"Go where?" Mary asked.

"James!"

"Dianne!"

"Go where? Do you know where my parents went?"

"We think they are buried in the rubble where your house used to be," Jackson said.

"Jackson!"

"We need to get my brother. He is in the hay beside our house," Mary said.

"I understand dear," Dianne said.

"No, you don't."

"A three year old is telling me that I don't understand?" Di said in disbelief.

"My brother is in the hay and we have to get him out of there or he will die the way people are dying in the rubble. He will be hungry and wet and cold and we need to help him."

"James, could you stay with Mary for a bit while we go out and see what is going on at Ground Zero. We have to file a report for PPZ. Steve just emailed me and said that the militia are being sent in to guard the area where the bank is believed to be buried," Dianne said.

"Did they find anyone yet," Jackson asked.

"No, Steve says they are not looking yet for people, they are just looking at the bank site for important papers and whatever might be buried there," Di said.

"Are you serious?" Jackson said.

"Why wouldn't I be? James could you watch Mary while we go out," Dianne asked again.

"Certainly, and I have to go out I will get one of the staff to sit with her," James replied.

CHAPTER 5

Du Quartidi: 24. Ventôse 239 around 4:58:88:

"My God what is that scratching, thumping, gnawing sound?" George Smoothman asked.

"Sounds like rats," Jay replied. "I am so thirsty" Jay added.

"Drink this, Jay" Kevin suggested.

"Don't drink anything that smells like whiskey. Use some common sense. We are in a terrible situation. We are somewhere, we don't really know where. We got here, we really don't know how. Men order us about dressed like Nazis wearing clothes that were designed almost a hundred years ago."

"Since when did you care about fashion, George?" Jay asked looking amused.

"Since the word fascist is so close to the word fashion in the dictionary? And we are being forced to work 8 decimal hours in a 10 decimal day," Kevin interjected.

"Look guys, I am not joking. Sam is dead. We are going to be worked to death. We are slaves here. We are going to lose track of our regular time, and we have no way to measure it. All we have to see are those strange decimal clocks. We must stay alive for Sam and free ourselves from this oppression. As foreman I order everyone to put the team first not your personal needs," George replied.

"Easy for you to say. What happens if we die of thirst?" Kevin asked.

"We won't die of thirst. What I am suggesting is that we need to not ruin our chances to survive this by drinking their poison. The rats must know where water is. They are survive here, maybe we can too."

"Are you saying that the rats are smarter than we are?" Jay asked looking offended.

"No, I am saying that if the rats can find a way to live here there must be a source of water and food," George said.

"Anyway the guards left this for us, and it is free," Kevin said

"Nothing is free here. Drinking that stuff will only make everything worse."

"Well the rats are free, at least freer than us," Kevin replied.

"What do you think they did with Sam's body? They seemed in a huge hurry when they took it away," Jay wondered out loud.

Kevin and George glared at Jay.

"I don't think we need to torture ourselves. We have to stay positive. And sometimes ignorance is bliss. We had good time when all around us were bad times. Maybe the rats, and don't laugh, travel back and forth to Pitville from Mina. Maybe if we observe what they do or find where the openings are, we could make them bigger and hide in transport containers just the way they do," George said.

"Are we allowed to laugh now, Mr. Foreman?"

"Of course not. We have to take every option seriously."

"Even stupid ones?"

"Yes, especially the stupid ones. Don't forget what is under everything and behind everything, it is a sort of like a Paradise lost that never goes away but is covered with grit, cobwebs and…"

"Rats," Jay added.

"Exactly," George said.

CHAPTER 6

March 15th 2031, around 12:00 PM:

"Di, do you see what I see?"

"Jackson contact Steve and tell him we are ready to go live. I am about to engage with this guy."

"Okay, Boss."

"Sir, I was wondering if you could take a few minutes and tell us what it was like to climb out of Cold Feet Mountain's rubble?" Dianne asked the miner closest to her."

"It was pretty awful. We climbed up the coal seam and thought we were going to die. Hey, I know you, you are Dianne Black, is this live?""

"I am not sure. At the moment it isn't, but Jackson my cameraman is trying to get us live so the outside world can see the conditions here. You don't mind going live do you?" Dianne asked realizing that she had never asked that question before, even though during her long career she has asked tens of thousands of questions.

"Of course I am alive. What did you think I was; a ghost? Look lady don't you think I am freaked out enough? I am I so freaked out about how close I was to being dead. What I saw I don't ever want to remember. I have never felt so close to death in all my life. I was sure I was going to die down there," Stanley said as he fought his urge to cough.

"Well I meant …"

"What did you mean?" Stanley asked.

"Could you tell us your story, Mr…

"Mr. Goodwin, my name is Stanley Goodwin. I see that you are taking care of Mary Clarke. Is her family safe? Their house appears to be gone," Stanley said.

"We don't know. So her house is gone, that is what we suspected. We found Mary sitting on the rubble totally traumatized. We assumed that she was sitting on what was left of her house. She has been screaming at us, not all the time, but some of the time, that her brother is in the hay. She can't accept that he is gone."

"Did you look in the hay to actually see if he is there?"

"Of course not, the air quality is terrible. As far as I know the rockslide and the deceased are going to be left undisturbed," Dianne said.

"They sure aren't leaving the bank site undisturbed, are they? We better go check. The militia will be here soon and they will make everything impossible. My guess is that they will guard the bank site for a while. Put a gate around it or something while claiming it is too dangerous to rescue or recover people who are underneath. Watch them turn the entire site into a museum and charge money to see and touch the rubble while selling ice cream and coffees," Stanley said cynically as he coughed uncontrollably. He took out his orange puffer and inhaled his medication deeply.

"I suppose no one will ever be sure who or what is under the rubble. If a person is not walking around by now, we can assume they are buried under all that rock," Dianne said noticeably shaken by Stanley's abrupt manner.

"David is just around a year old and would never be able to walk to safety on his own. We better see if he is there or he will become just another invisible and innocent victim of Coaltonstone's greed. They can go on and blame our depopulation on the cruelty of nature, but it is impossible to ignore the cruelty of that man," Stanley said.

"Mathew please change the channel. We don't need to be listening to Fake News," James said as Mathew obeyed.

"No one listens to us. No one listened to Mary. We should check the hay. She tried to tell you that her brother is in the hay probably because she saw him in there. Did anyone think of checking?"

"Mary is only three years old and appears to be severely traumatized," Dianne said.

"Why can't you answer me. Has anyone checked to see if David is in the hay?" Stanley asked again.

"No, we haven't," Dianne replied.

"They are checking the bank site and taking whatever they can before the militia get here. Why didn't they check the hay?" Stanley asked as he started to run for the hay stack, hoping that it was still there.

"At the time... I really don't think any baby could have been thrown into a pile of hay during the rockslide," Dianne as she motioned to Jackson to keep up with Stanley.

"Mary was thrown onto the pile of rubble. It probably is not impossible that her brother was thrown somewhere too," Jackson said before he ducked Dianne's glare and ran after Stanley trying not to bounce his camera too much.

"And no one thought to check the hay? We miners are survivors and take care of our own. We would all be dead if it wasn't for us standing up for our selves and finding ways to escape disaster after disaster, none of us would be alive today if we listened to our masters," Stanley yelled as he continued to run. Curious onlookers began to run behind Stanley, some commenting how unfair the establishment is to miners.

"Hold on you said there were twenty-six miners including yourself, but I count sixteen men, besides yourself," Dianne asked.

"So the miners who are deportees were shoveling the coal into the containers and two of the resident miners when outside for a lunch break," Stanley yelled back.

"And then what happened?

"We heard screams, and the liquid rock buried us and the men who were having their lunch outside must have been buried alive."

"You didn't answer my question, what happened to the chain gang of deportees?" Dianne asked again while raising her voice.

"What do you think happened to them? Some may have escaped. Who do you think will be chasing after them. You and Pretty Boy with his fancy camera?"

"Sir, you sound so angry and you are scaring me. We have nothing to do with this," Dianne said as she started to cry. "We are just telling people, my loyal viewers what the truth is," Dianne said as she motioned to Jackson to keep running.

"I am sorry if I sound rough. My night was one of the roughest nights of my life, and we don't have any time to waste making reality shows. If David is really in the hay he will be dying as we speak," Stanley said as he sprinted in the direction of the hay pile."

"Steve can you hear me, keep this live," Dianne ordered

"Dianne, should we be really putting this out live when we have no idea what we are going to find. The boy might not be there or he may be dead, even mutilated. Maybe we should screen what we put out before G.O.D. does it for us, permanently," Jackson said in protest.

"What do you have against reality? That is what we do."

"Jackson steady, now," Dianne said. "The hay is still here, pretty amazing.

"I don't hear anything, I thought if a baby was in that pile of hay he would be crying," Dianne said.

"Hold on, I think I can feel something," Stanley said.

"Jackson keep it rolling,"

"I got him, I got him," Stanley said. "I have to put him down and check to see if any mud or anything is blocking his breathing.

CHAPTER 7

March 15th 2031, around 12:10 PM:

"Uncle James, I thought you said we were going to the land bridge," Mathew said.

"Yes, there it is, right over there. The bridge is right over there. Can't you see it Mathew? Isn't it splendid? We are witnessing the connecting of Eurasia and North America. We are now entering a new era of trade and human development. I can see it and I am certainly more than twice your age."

"I see oil rig bots but I don't see any land bridge," Mathew said.

"That is because you are not looking in the right direction. It is not a land bridge, it is an under land bridge. My bridge tunnels below the sea and channels and connects to the military zone in Mina. Imagine all my coal and precious metals being transported under the land inside an almost invisible structure connecting Eurasia with North America, and all tariff free. Imagine the opportunities. This is a historic moment son. This moment defies what has been. Where we stand will be the path to a bridge that can change everything. My tunnels will expand into a glorious New World Power. When little James is your age he might never know war or terrorism nor world hunger and conflict. Expanding trade and improving distribution and production…"

"Uncle James I don't see any humans. I just see robots. I see lots of robots. How will humans get to get jobs at that construction site when only robots are being hired? I don't see any humans at all."

"Son don't be so cynical. This bridge could bring hope and peace to the entire human race will be all that little James will know. All the conflicts that we are living today, will be ancient history when James is your age. One day I will have a train system, which will transport everything the world needs to everywhere. No border, no wars, no tariffs."

"I thought we were at war with Mina."

"They are, I am not. The world is a strange place, and all kinds of people make very strange bedfellows. The unofficial reason we are at war, I mean they are at war with Mina is because Mina is threatening to demand that we pay all the money we owe them, and if we did that, our economy would collapse. Of course that is not the official reason. My Bot Dollar System could solve that problem too. All we need is a new currency that people trust, and with my face on every Botbill, how could they not trust such a currency especially when they see the words "In James Coaltonstone we trust.""

"This under land bridge just as good as any overland bridge, if not better, than the one we have in Coalton Valley One."

"I heard that you are going bankrupt, Uncle James. Is that true?

"Yes and no. Going bankrupt is not a bad thing. It is not me that is going bankrupt just a few of my holdings. You see Mathew I haven't and won't be losing everything. I still have assets."

"Like what?'

"My mines, my mineral rights, my offshore accounts."

"So why are they saying you are bankrupt?"

"Some of my holdings are going through bankrupt proceedings but that is a good thing. The loss of the river that was flowing into Bering Sea and is now flowing into the Pacific, well that is going to have a serious impact on our production in the present but in the future my surplus from my other holdings will have grown, tax free."

"Uncle James. I don't understand, what do you mean?" I still have my Botbills, and people are mining them, and my machinery is pushing ownership of them," James explained.

"Is that what IQ does? I was looking for him today and I couldn't find him."

"Yes mostly, he is locked in my Botbill mining room. The currency is mine. The currency is private. The machines needed to mine my Botbills are in circulation and are earning me a mint. The beauty is all this, is that the supply is fixed of both machines and currency are fixed. I control how low the floor can sink. When customers mine my Botbills while forming a new algorithm from the old one, they raise the ceiling value, whenever there is a frenzy of mining Botbills, I win," James Coaltonstone explained.

"How, Uncle James?"

"I, as the earliest and only founder will benefit the most as my new currency gains value. The Bot Botbill miners buy my machines to mine new Botbills, and they buy my machines from me. IQ's job is to monitor the progress of the Botbill mining machine algorithms and to maintain incentives for players to continue mining for me."

CHAPTER 8

March 15th 2031, around 1:00 PM:

"Hold on, Jethro, you need to start over, and please don't shout," Mayor Stern said as he turned his phone speakers on.

"Hi Jethro. Is Bill there too?" Susan asked.

"Yes, and we are in big trouble," Jethro said as he started to shout again.

"Jethro, you need to calm down. Your shouting is making my end crack up. Take a deep breath. Now start from the very beginning," Mayor Stern said as he rolled his eyes in Susan's direction.

"Bill blew up a rare whale when it was transmitting sonar signals by mistake thinking that it was an enemy sub, and now our cover has been blown. We are no longer under cover, we have ascended to the surface, and Bill is arguing with Richette Fauxto while a bunch of hippie protestors look as if they are in shock," Jethro explained.

"Protestors always look like that. Richette Fauxto is still alive? I remember when I was a boy I had a poster of her wearing nothing but boots plastered on my wall," Mayor Stern said." What is she doing there?" Mayor Stern asked looking amused.

"Ms. Fauxto told Bill that she is a passenger on the protestor's boat. She is observing the plight of the polar bears but from today she has expanded her mission to include saving the whales from fools like him," Jethro said.

"I have no idea why I thought she was dead," Mayor Stern said.

"Sir, aren't you listening? Richette Fauxto saw the whole thing, which probably means the explosion has been filmed. I think we need to stay on track here," Alex Coaltonstone said. "We don't need another incident. These situations are hurting our brand and are costing us a fortune in lawsuits. Jethro, Bill, your timing could not have been worse. The fake news people are making us look like villains and they are turning that Stanley Goodwin into a hero."

"Who is Stanley Goodwin? Is he related to Ginger Goodwin?" Jethro asked.

"Look we need to keep on track. As head of security the issues I am dealing with are overwhelming and the last thing we need is another incident. There are serious commotions at the bank site. The militia has been told to use live ammunition on the protestors that are getting out of hand.

"What did they expect was going to happen after they found captive deportees in the bank vault? I mean that Dianne Black managed to get that on live too almost instantaneously as she was making Stanley Goodwin into a hero while he was resuscitating that poor little boy they found in the hay," Susan said.

"You see, Jethro and Bill, your timing could not have been worse. Did anyone else see anything?" Mayor Stern asked.

"A small craft or a drone or something above our location. Whatever it was, it appeared to be taking photos or videos of the whales just before Bill made his tactical error," Jethro said. "Bill you are such a moron," Jethro added.

"Hold on Jethro, you were the one who told me to shoot. It was your fault, not mine," Bill said.

"I was about to ask, before I was so rudely interrupted by you fools, how much did Richette Fauxto see?" Mayor Stern asked.

"She has whale splattered all over her, and she is pretty upset. She has a film crew with her of course," Bill replied.

"At least there is one good outcome," Jethro said.

"And you think this is funny?" John Bell asked. "Do you realize how volatile our situation is right now. Do you realize how hard my job is getting. Even some of the members of the militia are considering walking over to the other side. That is all we need; trained soldiers fighting beside miners."

"All I meant was that the protestors have whale all over themselves, their boat and their equipment," Jethro explained.

"Jethro is right. The protestors and Richette Fauxto have whale all over them, sir, it is a real mess and very hard not to laugh when you look at their faces."

"The last thing we need to be doing is antagonising these people," Alex Coaltonstone said. "It will hurt our brand. Could even lead to a boycott.

"The protestors are really upset and Richette Fauxto is furious. Should we use our water hoses on them or should we just shoot them," Jethro asked.

"Jethro, you are joking with us, right?" Susan asked.

"No Mam. I don't joke," Jethro said while maintaining a stony looking face.

"Jethro doesn't joke," Bill interjected. "Sometimes I wish he would joke around, he would be a lot easier to work and live with," Bill added.

"Descend. Get inside your boat and descend. Navigate back to the military zone. If the protestors follow you they will be arrested, and treated like every other illegal," Mayor Stern said.

"Good idea," Bill said.

And how are the illegals being treated?" Susan asked.

"The authorities shave their heads and put them in stripes and teach them to respect authority," Jethro said as he fought an involuntary grin."

"Are you kidding me?" Susan asked.

"You don't want to know," Jethro replied.

"While you descend, tell us what happened one more time, and Susan listen carefully while you take notes."

"You are sure you want me to take notes? You told me not to take notes."

"That is my job, to know when to tell you to take notes and when not to take notes because I am the head of security and you are a secretary or something like that," John Bell said.

"Didn't you do a great job protecting Ginger and your brother? You managed to shoot Ginger and your brother got shot when someone thought he was you," Susan said in disgust.

"You two, cut it out," Mayor Stern ordered.

"Jethro and I aren't doing anything. We are waiting for our turn to speak. Is it our turn to speak yet?" Bill asked.

"Of course; that is the point of this entire meeting," Mayor Stern said.

"I understand. Well, we had sonar contact so we assumed it was a spy sub, and blew it up."

"Jethro, you astonish me," Mayor Stern said.

"Yes, sir, the whole event was very astonishing. There was whale oil everywhere, sir," Jethro said as he waved his big hairy hands in the air.

"No one was more astonished than we were, sir, except maybe that boy that was flyking up directly above the whale. He looked rather traumatised. He had been filming the creature right before we blew it up," Bill explained as he stared into the computer cam.

"Didn't it even dawn on you that it could have been a whale using echolocation to find food or other whales?" Susan asked while she continued to type.

"No, we thought we were in harms way. We are trained to engage with the enemy when we come in sonar contact. We took action to protect our boat and our crew," Jethro explained without offering an apology.

"Jethro you blew up a whale in front of Richette Fauxto of all people," Susan said.

"We are at war, Mam," Bill added.

"Now let's start over again. Start from the very beginning, you Jethro, you go first, tell us how you thought you were aiming for enemy subs and actually blew up a rare whale in the Bering Sea. And please, Jethro, don't leave out any detail," John Bell ordered.

"Why me, why not let Bill explain first. He was the one who shot the whale," Jethro said.

"Yes but it was you who gave the authorization for Bill to shoot the whale," Mayor Stern said.

"James Coaltonstone is horrified that another 'incident' is going to place the Big Seven Coal Group under scrutiny again," John Bell added.

"Well you are one to talk, you shot Ginger Goodwin. And almost every miner on Tut Island and beyond were either surrounding the security fence in protest or were burning tires the Coalton Valley Parkway," Bill said accusingly.

"I thought we put all that behind us," Mayor Stern said.

"That will be the day," Susan whispered.

"They will never let me put this horrible situation behind me. I am the victim. I was forced to defend myself from Ginger Goodwin. I am going to be haunted by this for the rest of my life and probably for even longer than that," John Bell said.

"Well at least you are alive. I have never seen Ginger with anything more threatening than that tube cased he used to carry with his reports in it," Susan said.

"No one cares that he was pointing something at me that appeared to be a rifle of some sort and I shot him in self-defense," John Bell said.

"Ginger was a pacifist. He was protesting because he was objecting to being drafted. He was refusing to kill the very men who helped him escape from Mine Five when our own men were still waiting for the perfect time to help him," Susan said as she continued to type.

"Whose side are you one, woman?" John Bell asked Susan.

"Come on, you guys," Jethro said. "This is supposed to be a meeting about how we torpedoed a whale by mistake, and you know I think it was an honest mistake. We had no idea if it was a whale or the enemy using old sonar technology. We only had a fraction of a second to make a decision," Bill said.

"That is exactly the position that I was in. I had a fraction of a second to decide how to respond," John Bell said. "I wasn't even expecting to come across him. I thought he would have left the island. How was I to know he was in the mountain bush," John Bell said.

"Well, you should have known. You were chasing him. You and those skin heads you hang out with," Susan said.

"Susan! Really!" Mayor Stern interjected. "This meeting is about the whale killing not about Ginger being shot."

"Yes sir," Susan said.

"I only had a fraction of second to make a decision, sir. What if it had been an enemy submarine, we instead of that whale could have been splattered to smithereens," Jethro said. "Then what would the survivors think then?

"Well, someone is pretty upset with you, John. And they haven't caught him yet. So I can understand how you feel. Whoever it was who shot Don, he must have thought it was you," Bill said.

"Even though clearly Don was the better looking twin," Jethro added.

"What do you think it is like for me. Every time I look in the mirror it feels like I am looking at Don," John said.

"That is pretty stupid, Don was the far better looking than you," Bill retorted.

"What made you think that Ginger would shoot anyone? Knowing Ginger he was probably just carrying reports or something in his tube-case."

"We need to be discussing why you blew up the whale," Mayor Stern interjected.

"We torpedoed the whale and we blew it up because we thought that it was an enemy sub. Whale was splattered all over the place. It was very messy. The protestors were pretty upset," Bill said.

"End of story," Jethro added.

"We already know all this. What aren't you telling us?" Mayor Stern asked.

"Sir, shouldn't we be discussing the costing of security in Pitville? We have protestors hanging out on Cold Feet Mountain who are just as furious as the protestors who are hanging out in Pitville except they seem to be helping the rescue effort," Alex Coaltonstone said.

"You mean they are rescuing the loot at the bank site?" John Bell asked.

"Both. They found a baby boy in hay and some are looting the bank site," Alex Coaltonstone replied.

"It was actually Stanley Goodwin who found the little Clarke boy, and it was streamed live. It is a miracle that boy survived," Susan said.

"I didn't know that there was a rescue effort was in progress. I received the memo from G.O.D., which appeared to clearly state that the rescue effort could only be treated as a recovery effort, and to rush its execution might put rescuers in harm's way," Mayor Stern said.

"Sounds exactly like the memo we got when Ginger was trapped in Mine Five," Susan said. "The Minese miners were the only ones who were able to rescue Ginger. George, Jay, Sam and Kevin tried to rescue Ginger too, but we have no idea what happened to them. They seem to have vanished into thin air," Susan said.

"Excuse me; my wife is on the phone." Mayor Stern said.

"Certainly," Susan replied.

"What do you mean your car is broken? What happened?"

"The mechanic said that there are rats in my car and they have eaten some of the wires in my car. I could have been killed. There was a small fire in my car."

"I will be there right away, dear," Mayor Stern said.

"You don't sound surprised," Mrs. Stern said.

"It seems to be happening all over town," Mayor Stern replied.

CHAPTER 9

March 15th 2031, around 2:00 PM:

"No!" James said as he thumped his fist on Mayor Stern's desk startling Susan who dropped the tray off coffee all over him.

"Losses are difficult, James. We have had so many," Mayor Stern said. "G.O.D. is just requiring a short inspection before the mine is allowed to re-open; just a formality, really. And Susan try to be more careful when serving the coffee," Mayor Stern said.

"I am so sorry sir," Susan said.

"Everything is going wrong today, I think I will take up my step son's offer and go flyking with him," James said.

"Sir, d"Losses are difficult, James. We have had so many," Mayor Stern said. "G.O.D. is just requiring a short inspection before the mine is allowed don't you think you are rather old to go flyking?"

"Susan," Mayor Stern interjected.

"I certainly I am not," James retorted.

"What about the weather? James, those black clouds could really hamper your visibility," Mayor Stern warned.

"You know I need a holiday. My stepson says flyking is the most heavenly sport there is and I feel at the moment as if I am trapped in the worst hellhole known to man," James complained.

"Pitville is a beautiful town," Mayor Stern said.

"Dad, let's be perfectly frank, you are older and you could get hurt and the city life insurance would be void," Alex Coaltonstone explained.

"Since when did Pitville acquire this life insurance policy?" James asked as he sat down looking deflated.

"We acquired it last week," Susan said.

"So I can't go flyking?" James asked looking shocked.

"I am afraid not, it is a forbidden activity at the moment. It is just too much risk for the insurance company to carry. We were lucky we could get a life insurance policy on you. We would be lost without you, you know," Mayor Stern said.

"So if something happened to me, how much would you get?"

"A thousand million," Susan said.

"You mean a billion?" James asked.

"Yes, a billion," Susan replied.

"You have to admit we are losing one key person after another. If we lost you…" Mayor Stern said before James interrupted him.

"What am I supposed to say to my step son?" James asked.

"Tell him the truth," Susan suggested.

"Good advice Susan," Mayor Stern said giving Susan a nod.

"Dad, don't you think flyking is awfully dangerous for a many your age? Everyone else does," Alex Coaltonstone asked.

"Alex," Susan scolded.

"I thought we were telling the truth," Alex said defensively. "I am sorry Dad, if I hurt your feelings, I didn't mean to." Alex glared at Susan.

"I understand son. If you were my age, you probably would be too old to flyke. You are just an accountant and I am an entrepreneur," James said as he laughed. "I am kidding son. I am, really I am."

"I would really miss you James if anything happened to you. With the war and all I just think flyking is dangerous and too much of a risk. I am surprised Maria isn't worried sick when Mathew is out there flyking all by himself," Susan said sounding stressed out.

"Maria goes flyking with Mathew, but since the accident, Mathew has wanted to stay with me on the ship to be close to his mother, his brother and Doctor Knight," James explained. "I guess I will have to phone and explain it to him," James added. "Pardon me."

"Certainly, James, you take your time, or even better suggest something safer to do like bowling," Mayor Stern suggested.

"Hello, is that you Mathew, I have some bad new," James said.

"Oh now, did someone just get hurt or killed again?" Mathew asked.

"No, I suppose in perspective, this news is not so bad," James replied.

"So, what is the problem?"

"Mathew, I can't go flyking with you but would you like to go bowling instead and maybe go for a bite to eat after?" James asked.

"Why can't you go flyking with me?"

"I am not allowed to," James said sheepishly.

"I don't believe that. You are James Coaltonstone, you are supposed to be able to do whatever you want and whenever you want," Mathew said.

"Well, sometimes the rules change on people unexpectedly and we just have to adapt. I was told that the life insurance that the city carries on my me does not allow me to Flyke or do any extreme sports," James said. "We had a meeting and I was also told I was too old to go flyke and maybe we should go bowling instead," James said.

"I don't believe this. How could you not be allowed to do anything? You are James Coaltonstone. I will just go flyking by myself if you don't want to go with me. How can they say you are too old to go flyking? You are not as old as grandma are you?"

"I am certainly not that old," James agreed.

"If Grandma can go flyking with me, why can't you?"

"The city has a life insurance policy on me and I would be voiding it if I participate in extreme sports," James said. "We could go bowling, would you like that?" James added.

"I just don't believe it," Mathew said then hung up.

James left city hall wondering if he should just go flyking and damn the life insurance policy. It wasn't like he was the one who bought it or chose to have it.

CHAPTER 10

March 17th 2031, around 12:00 AM:

"I can't believe it. You shot my step-son by mistake? Where is he now? Is he badly injured?

"They are looking for him in the water, sir," Jethro replied. "He just fell out of the air and disappeared into the water, sir."

"How could you have shot my stepson as if he were a bird or a drone or something?" James asked.

"It was a terrible accident sir. I thought he was a drone, sir."

"Hold on I am getting a phone call," James said.

"He landed in the water. We haven't been able to locate him. I really did think that he was a drone, sir."

"I am talking to Mathew's grandmother on the phone, could you please shut up," James said.

"Of course I didn't mean you Maria; I meant the numbskull who shot your grandson while he was flyking."

"You don't understand, sir, it wasn't my fault. The weather was terrible. Black clouds and birds were all over the sky. We were sent a red alert that an enemy drone was spying on our ship."

"You thought my stepson was a drone? You didn't notice his mechanical feathers and reflective vest?"

"No. The black clouds were blocking our view, sir. All I saw were the lights from his camera so I thought that he was a drone, sir."

"James, I will be there in a few hours," Maria said.

"That won't be necessary," James said.

"Yes it is. I promised to help Dianne with those poor children. Jackson and Dianne got married at a civil ceremony in the hotel. Dianne grabbed a couple of witnesses from the elevator. Both Jackson's and Dianne's parents are upset they weren't invited to the wedding so they asked me to help with the kids. G.O.D. has approved Dianne's application to adopt and she has her hands full. And keeping will help me. I sit around thinking of losing Mathew, his dad, his mom, Ginger and little Ginger junior fighting for his life. Ginger's friends, George, Jay, Sam and Kevin, still missing and no one knows where they are. It seems the only people who are getting ahead are the type of men who kill innocent people," Maria said.

"That is not entirely true Maria. Jethro is so fired. Do you hear me Jethro, you are FIRED."

"I know Maria, it is one loss after another and I know one mistake after another too. I don't know what to say. We just don't know where Mathew is."

"James is it the same man who shot that poor whale to bits," Maria asked.

"No, that was his partner, Bill. Actually it was Jethro who gave Bill the instructions to blow up the whale."

"Oh my God, what is wrong with you people? Even you James, whoever you love seems to fall under some terrible curse of bad luck."

"Maria cut it out."

"I know James, it is not fair. But it seems true. Whatever you do seems to turn people's luck against them. The more a person's luck is turned against them the more you seem to thrive. Why is that? It is as if you personify food chain economics," Maria said.

"I have to go. I can't talk about this anymore. I am going to launch a search party and see if we can find Mathew. I certainly don't believe that Mathew was shot to bits like the whale was. I will phone you back as soon as I can, Maria," James Added.

"Jethro, did you actually see Mathew land in the water?"

"Sir, my lawyer is on the other line and I am being advised to let him do the talking. I am sorry sir, I have to go."

THE END

STAY TUNED FOR BOOK 5

Produced by S.E. McKenzie Productions
First Print Edition May 2017

Enquiries:

Email Address:
messidartha@aol.com

http://www.amazon.com/SarahMcKenzie/e/B00H9RWX48/